MR.
DAYDREAM

by Roger Hargreaves

This is a story about Mr Daydream.

You know what he looks like don't you, because you've seen his picture on the front of this book.

It's also a story about a little boy called Jack.

And you don't know what he looks like, so here's a picture of him.

Now Jack was a very good little boy.

He always ate up all his lunch.

He always went to bed when he was told.

He always said 'Please' and 'Thank you'.

But Jack was a daydreamer!

Whenever he was supposed to bethinking about something, he found himself thinking about something else.

Daydreaming!

One day, Jack was at school.

He was sitting at his desk listening to the teacher talking about history.

It was a very warm day and Jack was glad he was sitting at the back of the classroom next to the open window.

Suddenly, out of the corner of his eye, Jack saw something outside the window on the grass in front of the school.

Something blue!

It was a small, cloud-shaped figure.

Jack couldn't believe his eyes.

The figure looked at Jack looking at him, smiled and waved.

Jack looked at his teacher who was still talking.

Then he got up quietly, ever so quietly, and slipped out of the open window.

He crossed the grass to the strange-looking cloud-shaped figure.

"Hello," he said. "Who are you?"

"I'm Mr Daydream," said the figure. "What's your name?"

"Jack," said Jack.

"I'm going off on an adventure," said Mr Daydream to Jack. "Would you like to come with me?"

"Oh, yes please," replied Jack.

"Very well then," said Mr Daydream and, putting two fingers in his mouth, he let out the loudest whistle Jack had ever heard in his whole life.

A huge bird swooped down out of the sky and landed beside Jack and Mr Daydream.

"Come on," said Mr Daydream to Jack, and climbed onto the bird's back.

Jack climbed on too. It was a really enormous bird, and there was plenty of room for both of them.

"Hold on," said Mr Daydream.

Jack held on tight.

The huge bird flapped its huge wings, and suddenly they were high up in the air.

They flew faster and faster over the countryside.

They flew over fields and farms and towns and hills and trees and valleys until they were far far away from Jack's school.

It was very exciting!

Mr Daydream turned to Jack.

"How would you like to go to Africa?" he shouted.

They were travelling so fast now, Jack just nodded his head, and held on even tighter.

And they flew and they flew across the sea.

Suddenly, it seemed in no time at all, there below them was Africa.

The bird landed in a jungle clearing, and Jack and Mr Daydream climbed off the bird's back.

It was very hot!

"Come on," said Mr Daydream to Jack. "Let's go and explore."

So off they set, pushing their way through the jungle.

Suddenly, in the middle of the clearing, they saw an elephant.

"Hello, Mr Daydream," trumpeted the elephant down its trunk. "Would you like a lift?"

"Yes please," replied Mr Daydream, and the elephant reached out his trunk, picked him up and then put him on his back. Then he reached out his trunk again, picked up Jack and put him on his back.

It was very high!

The elephant carried them through the jungle until they came to a river.

Then he set them down on the ground, said goodbye, and went off back into the jungle.

"How are we going to cross the river?" Jack asked Mr Daydream.

"Perhaps I can be of assistance," wheezed a particularly oily voice coming from the river.

They looked, and there was a crocodile.

"Use my back as a bridge," suggested the crocodile.

It was very helpful!

They were half way across the river on the crocodile's back when the crocodile grinned a rather nasty grin – all teeth and no smile.

Then, flicking his enormous tail, and shooting Jack and Mr Daydream up into the air, the crocodile opened his horribly large mouth, and waited.

It was very frightening!

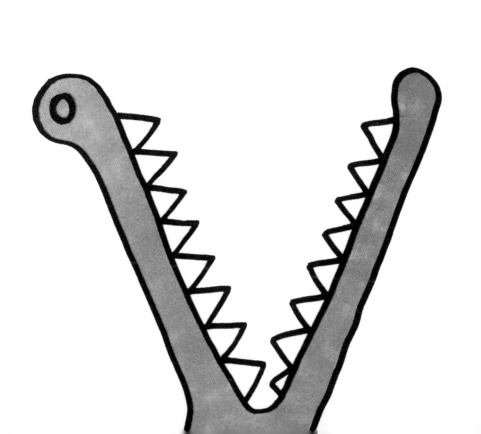

"Oh dear," gasped Jack as he looked down at that enormous mouthful of teeth. "Oh dear. Oh help!"

Mr Daydream, upside down beside him, put two fingers in his mouth and let out that very large whistle of his.

Suddenly, just as the crocodile's mouth was about to go SNAP, the big bird swooped down out of the sky.

Mr Daydream and Jack landed right on the bird's back.

"Whew!" said Jack.

"Bother!" said the crocodile.

"Well I promised you an adventure, didn't I?" grinned Mr Daydream.

"You certainly did," said Jack.

"And now," said Mr Daydream, "I think we will go to Australia."

And they did!

And Jack learned to throw a boomerang so that it always came back to him.

"And now," said Mr Daydream, "I think we will go to the North Pole."

And they did!

And Mr Daydream fell right up to his middle in a snowdrift!

"And now," said Mr Daydream, "I think we will go to the Wild West."

And they did!

And Mr Daydream found a huge, ten-gallon cowboy hat.

The trouble was, when he put it on, he couldn't see out.

"Jack," he called from underneath the hat.

"Jack!"

"Jack!"

Suddenly Jack realised that it wasn't Mr Daydream saying his name.

It was his teacher.

And Jack wasn't in the Wild West.

He was sitting at his school desk.

"Jack," said the teacher again. "You've been daydreaming!"

It was true.

He had.

But do you know something?

Daydreaming is more fun than history!